To

_____

From

_____

On this Date

_____

To Hayla, Daisy, Chloe, and Rebekah.
For all of the birthdays, and every occasion missed.
I love you very much—Papaw
—RC

Happy Birthday, FIONA

WITHDRAWN

NEW YORK TIMES BESTSELLING ILLUSTRATOR
RICHARD COWDREY

ZONDERKIDZ

Happy Birthday, Fiona
Copyright © 2022 by Zondervan
Illustrations © 2022 by Zondervan

Requests for information
should be addressed to:

Zonderkidz, 3900 Sparks Dr. SE,
Grand Rapids, Michigan 49546

Library of Congress Cataloging-in-Publication Data
Names: Cowdrey, Richard, author, illustrator.
Title: Happy birthday, Fiona / Richard Cowdrey.
Description: Grand Rapids, Michigan : Zonderkidz, 2022. | Audience: Ages
4-8. | Summary: It is Fiona's birthday, and fans from all over the world
are sending her cards and gifts, she is giving interviews and having her
picture taken, and with all the fuss she is neglecting her zoo
friends--and when her mother points this out she decides to throw her
own party, with gifts for all her animal friends.
Identifiers: LCCN 2021023928 | ISBN 9780310751649 (hardcover) | ISBN
9780310751663 (ebook)
Subjects: LCSH: Fiona (Hippopotamus), 2017---Juvenile fiction. |
Hippopotamus--Juvenile fiction. | Zoo animals--Juvenile fiction. |
Birthday parties--Juvenile fiction. | Friendship--Juvenile fiction. |
CYAC: Hippopotamus--Fiction. | Zoo animals--Fiction. |
Birthdays--Fiction. | Parties--Fiction. | Friendship--Fiction.
Classification: LCC PZ7.1.C685 Hap 2022 | DDC [E]--dc23
LC record available at https://lccn.loc.gov/2021023928

Illustrated by: Richard Cowdrey
        Contributors: Barbara Herndon and Mary Hassinger
Art direction and design: Cindy Davis

Printed in Korea

22 23 24 25 /SAM/ 20 19 18 17 16 15 14 13 12 11 10 9 8 7 6 5 4 3 2 1

It was a chilly day at the zoo, but warm wishes were in the air as everyone was getting ready for Fiona the Hippo's birthday!

Fiona was growing up and fans from all over the world
were sending birthday wishes to their favorite little hippo.

Bags and boxes and bouquets of every shape and size were
being delivered by trucks and vans to the zoo.

"Wow! People are so nice to me ... Oh! Look at the fruit bouquet!"
squealed Fiona as another delivery person dropped
off a load of cards and gifts to Hippo Cove.

Fiona's animal friends at the zoo were just as excited about Fiona's birthday.

They CHITTERED and CHATTERED about the big day.

"It's so exciting!"

"It sure is!"

"I think we need to do something too."

"Let's throw a party!!"

"That's a great idea!"

The animals got busy with the party preparations.
Some made signs and an invitation for Fiona.

Others made cards and gifts for their favorite little hippo.
"Fiona's going to be SO EXCITED!" squealed Flamingo.

The party was all set. The signs and gifts were made, and it was time to invite their guest of honor.

But every time the animals went to find Fiona and give her the invitation, she was busy!

Busy posing for birthday photos ...
"CHEESE!!"

Busy wading through the bags of fan mail ... "Dear Fiona, you are amazing!"

Busy trying out her new skateboard ... "Weeeeeeeeeeeee!"

"It sure looks like Fiona's having a great birthday," whispered Bear.
"I wonder if she'll have time for *our* party?" questioned Otter.

Fiona was suddenly whisked away for another photoshoot out in her pool.
"Hi, guys! Bye, guys!" she called out to her friends.

"Let's go, everyone," Giraffe whispered as the animals headed home.
"Fiona doesn't have time for us today."

Fiona was having FUN! She paddled and blew bubbles
and bobbed in the water as the cameras flashed. And
people cheered, "There's the birthday girl!"

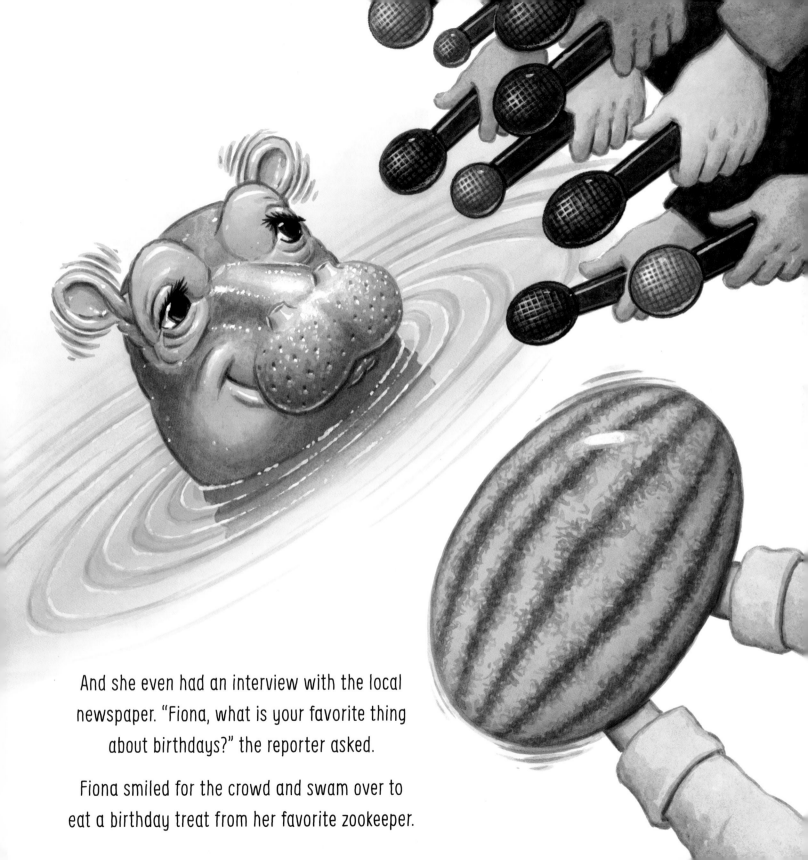

And she even had an interview with the local newspaper. "Fiona, what is your favorite thing about birthdays?" the reporter asked.

Fiona smiled for the crowd and swam over to eat a birthday treat from her favorite zookeeper.

Later that day, as Fiona was looking at more cards and letters, she stopped and glanced around the room. It felt as if something was missing ... what was it?

Fiona moved on to her pile of new toys. As the little birthday hippo rode in her shiny new red wagon, she had that feeling again. Something was missing. She looked around the room again and suddenly she knew! It wasn't **something** that was missing, it was **someone**. Where were all her animal friends?

Where is everyone? Fiona thought to herself as she walked past stacks of gifts and cards and treats.

The bananas and grapes were Monkey's favorite. Where was he? Seal would LOVE the new red exercise ball.

And the meerkats would certainly want to use the new beach pail and shovels!

HAPPY BIRTHDAY FIONA

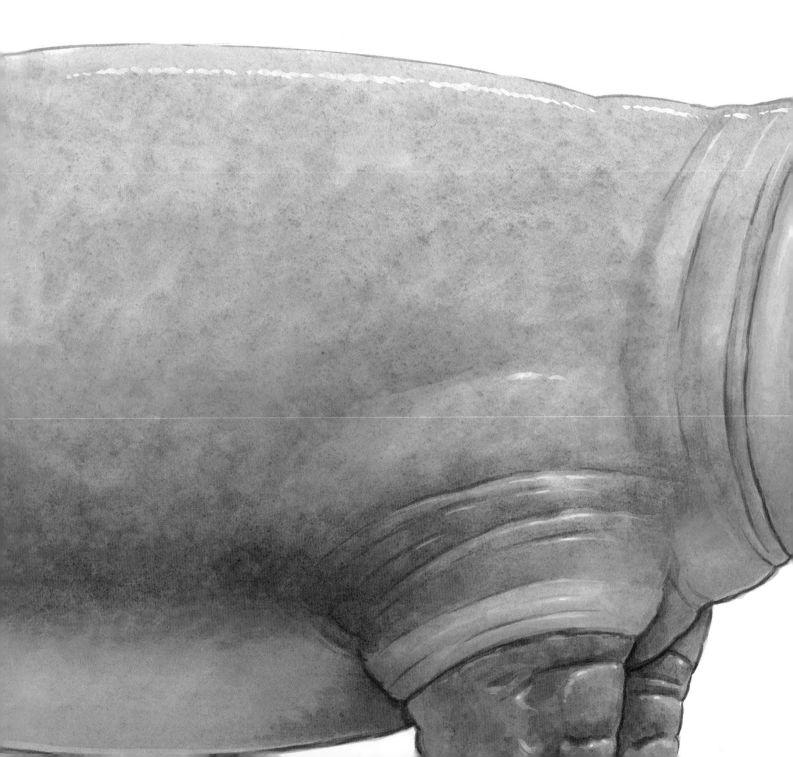

Fiona shared her feelings with Mama.
"None of my friends have come to play. Why don't
they want to see my new things?" she asked.

"You've been very busy, Fiona," Mama said.
"Have you invited anyone over?"

Fiona thought a minute. "My friends know
they can come here anytime."

"Sometimes it is nice to be asked,"
Mama said gently.

And just then Fiona came up with a great idea ...

"Thanks, Mama! I've got this!" And off Fiona went.

Fiona made party invitations
for all her friends.

"A birthday party?"

"I can't wait!"

"For me?"

"Don't be late!"
squealed an excited Fiona.

Fiona ran home and gathered up all her gifts—the balls, the shovels, the treats, the flowers, the books, the cars and wagons and pool floaties and noodles. Everything was ready and waiting. Fiona was happier than ever!

One by one, Fiona's friends arrived at the party.

"Wow, look at all those presents!"

"And yummy treats!"

"You sure are lucky, Fiona!"

"You're right, I am lucky," replied Fiona.
"But these presents aren't for me—
they're for all of you!"

The animals went WILD with excitement as Fiona handed out the gifts.

"For me?"

"Fiona! This is amazing!"

"Look, I can see myself!"

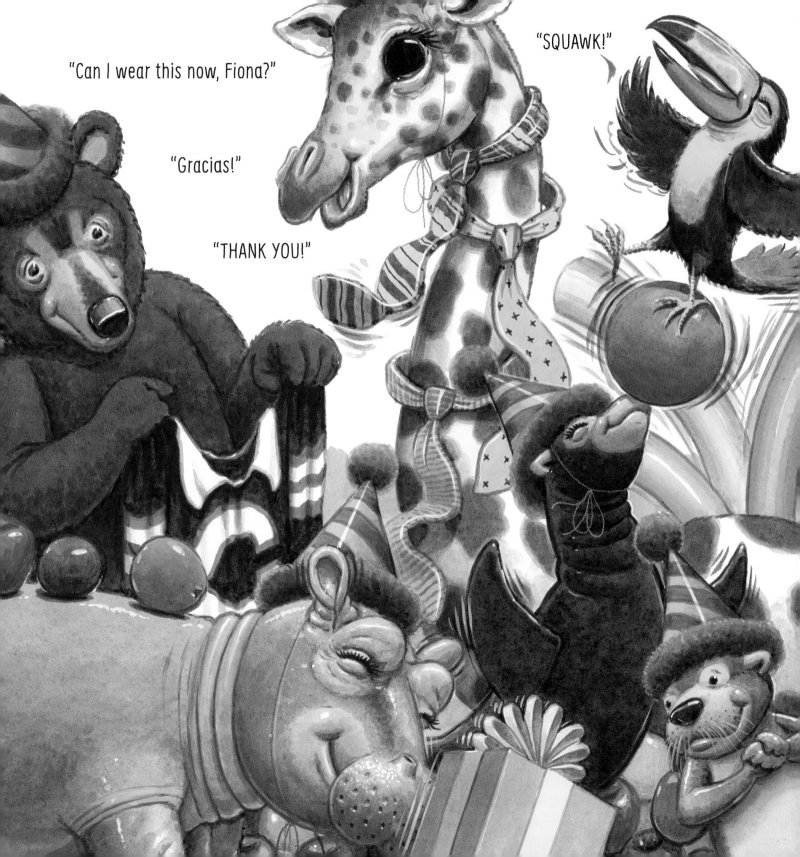

As everyone played with their party gifts, Fiona had one last surprise— a birthday cake made especially for Fiona and her animal friends!

"Make a birthday wish, Fiona!"

"That's okay," she replied. "Having all of you here means my wish has already come true. Now, dig in, everyone!!!"

"Mmmmm, cake!"

"Happy Birthday, my storied little hippo. How does it feel to be a year older?" asked Mama.

"It's a lot of work growing up ... but it feels good," replied Fiona.

"Speaking of work, when are you going to send out your thank you notes?"

"Oh, Mama. Can I do it tomorrow?"

"Of course, you can. Sleep well, birthday girl."

And she did.